For Molly Melling
Thanks Mum

HODDER CHILDREN'S BOOKS

First published in Great Britain in 2004 by Hodder and Stoughton
This edition published in 2017

A CIP catalogue record for this book
is available from the British Library.

ISBN: 978 1 444 93179 2

10 9 8 7 6 5 4 3 2 1

Printed and bound in China

Hodder Children's Books
An imprint of Hachette Children's Group
Part of Hodder and Stoughton
Carmelite House
50 Victoria Embankment
London EC4Y ODZ

An Hachette UK Company
www.hachette.co.uk

www.hachettechildrens.co.uk

www.davidmelling.co.uk

JUST LIKE
MY MUMMY

DAVID MELLING

Hodder
Children's
Books

This is my mummy.

In the morning I always wake early,
just like my mummy.

I y-a-w-n,

and grrroan,

and I'm ready for the day,

just like my mummy.

  If I hurt myself,

or argue with
someone,

 or get upset,

my mummy makes
me feel better.

And when I'm a cheeky little monkey,

I say "sorry", just like my mummy.

When I'm bored my
mummy doesn't like it.

She says,
"Why don't you DO something?"

But when I do something she says,

My mummy helps
me make things.
She knows everything.

And her ideas are SO interesting...

...everyone
wants to play!

Sometimes I have good ideas of my own.

But Mummy says,

"Dry games are better!"

That's typical…

There's an old squiggly tree
which is my favourite place
for climbing with my friends.

At the end of the day, we all
want to be somewhere quiet,
safe and warm, with someone...

...just like my mummy.

LOOK OUT FOR THESE GREAT STORIES STARRING:

HUGLESS DOUGLAS

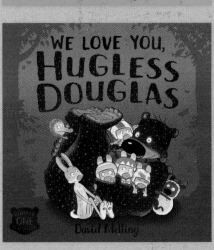

DON'T WORRY, **HUGLESS DOUGLAS**

David Melling

HUGLESS DOUGLAS and the BIG SLEEP

David Melling

WE LOVE YOU, **HUGLESS DOUGLAS**

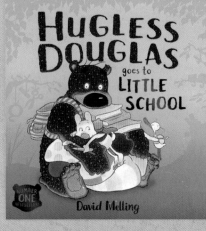
David Melling

HAPPY BIRTHDAY, **HUGLESS DOUGLAS**

David Melling

HUGLESS DOUGLAS goes to LITTLE SCHOOL

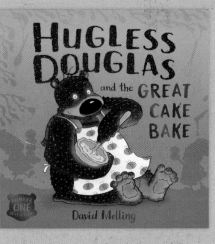
David Melling

HUGLESS DOUGLAS and the GREAT CAKE BAKE

David Melling